Samuel Foote

The Patron - A Comedy in Three Acts

As it is Performed at the Theatre in the Hay-market. Second Edition

Samuel Foote

The Patron · A Comedy in Three Acts
As it is Performed at the Theatre in the Hay-market. Second Edition

ISBN/EAN: 9783337067434

Printed in Europe, USA, Canada, Australia, Japan

Cover: Foto ©Andreas Hilbeck / pixelio.de

More available books at **www.hansebooks.com**

THE

PATRON.

A

COMEDY

IN THREE ACTS.

As it is Performed at the

THEATRE in the HAY-MARKET.

By SAMUEL FOOTE, Efq;

The SECOND EDITION.

LONDON,

Printed for G. KEARSLY, oppofite St. Martin's Church,
in Ludgate-Street.   1764.

Granville Levefon Gower,

Earl Gower, Lord Chamberlain of his Majefty's Houfhold.

My Lord,

THE following little comedy, founded on a ftory of M. Marmontelle's, and calculated to expofe the frivolity and ignorance of the pretenders to learning, with the infolence and vanity of their fuperficial, illiberal protectors, can be addreffed to no nobleman with more propriety than to Lord Gower; whofe judgment, though elegant, is void of affectation ; and whofe patronage, though powerful, is deftitute of all faftidious parade. It is with pleafure, my Lord, that the public fees your Lordfhip plac'd at the head of that department which is to decide, without appeal,

on

on the moſt popular domain in the whole
republic of letters ; a ſpot that has always
been diſtinguiſh'd with affection, and cul-
tivated with care, by every ruler the leaſt
attentive to either chaſtiſing the morals,
poliſhing the manners, or what is of equal
importance, rationally amuſing the leiſure
of the people.

The Patron, my Lord, who now begs
your protection, has had the good fortune
to be well receiv'd by the public ; and indeed, of all the pieces that I have had the
honour to offer them, this ſeems to me to
have the faireſt claim to their favour.

But the play, ſtripped of thoſe theatrical
ornaments for which it is indebted to your
Lordſhip's indulgence, muſt now plead it's
own cauſe ; nor will I, my Lord, with an
affected humility, echo the trite, coarſe,
though claſſical compliment, of Optimus
patronus peſſimus poeta : For if this be
really true of the laſt, the firſt can have but
ſmall pretenſions to praiſe ; patronizing bad
poets being, in my poor opinion, full as
pernicious to the progreſs of letters, as
neglecting the good.

In

In humble hopes, then, my Lord, of not being thought the meaneſt in the muſes train, I have taken the liberty to prefix your name to this dedication, and publickly to acknowlege my obligations to your lordſhip; which, let me boaſt too, I have had the happineſs to receive, untainted by the inſolence of domeſtics, the delays of office, or the chilling ſuperiority of rank; mortifications which have been too often experienced by much greater writers than myſelf, from much leſs men than your Lordſhip.

My Lord, I have the honour to be, with the greateſt reſpect and gratitude,

Your Lordſhip's moſt oblig'd,

and moſt devoted,

humble ſervant,

Weſt-End,
June 20, 1764.

SAMUEL FOOTE.

Dramatis Personæ.

Sir THOMAS LOFTY,	
Sir PETER PEPPERPOT,	} Mr. FOOTE.
DICK BEVER,	Mr. DEATH.
FRANK YOUNGER,	Mr. DAVIS.
Sir ROGER DOWLAS,	Mr. PALMER.
Mr. RUST,	Mr. WESTON.
Mr. DACTYL,	Mr. GRANGER.
Mr. PUFF,	Mr. HAYES.
Mr. STAYTAPE,	Mr. BROWN.
ROBIN,	Mr. PARSONS.
JOHN,	Mr. LEWIS.
Two Blacks.	
Miſs JULIET,	Mrs. GRANGER.

THE

PATRON.

ACT I.

Scene the Street.

Enter BEVER *and* YOUNGER.

YOUNGER.

O, Dick, you muſt pardon me.

BEVER.

Nay, but to ſatisfy your curioſity.

YOUNGER.

I tell you, I have not a jot.

BEVER.

Why then to gratify me.

B   YOUNGER.

YOUNGER.

At rather too great an expence.

BEVER.

To a fellow of your obfervation and turn, I fhould think now fuch a fcene a moft delicate treat.

YOUNGER.

Delicate ! Palling, naufeous, to a dreadful degree. To a lover, indeed, the charms of the niece may palliate the uncle's fulfome formality.

BEVER.

The uncle ! ay, but then you know he is only one of the group.

YOUNGER.

That's true ; but the figures are all finifh'd alike. A maniere, a tirefome famenefs throughout.

BEVER.

There you will excufe me ; I am fure there is no want of variety.

YOUNGER.

No ! then let us have a detail. Come, Dick, give us a bill of the play.

BEVER.

Firft, you know, there's Juliet's uncle.

YOUNGER.

What, Sir Thomas Lofty ! the modern Midas, or rather (as fifty dedications will tell

tell you) the Pollio, the Atticus, the patron of genius, the protector of arts, the paragon of poets, decider on merit, chief justice of taste, and sworn appraiser to Apollo and the tuneful nine. Ha, ha. Oh, the tedious, insipid, insufferable coxcomb!

BEVER.

Nay, now, Frank, you are too extravagant. He is universally allow'd to have taste ; sharp-judging Adriel, the muse's friend, himself a muse.

YOUNGER.

Taste ! by who ? underling bards, that he feeds ; and broken booksellers, that he bribes. Look ye, Dick, what raptures you please, when Miss Lofty is your theme, but expect no quarter for the rest of the family. I tell thee once for all, Lofty is a rank impostor, the bufo of an illiberal mercenary tribe ; he has neither genius to create, judgment to distinguish, or generosity to reward ; his wealth has gain'd him flattery from the indigent, and the haughty insolence of his pretence, admiration from the ignorant. Voila lè portrait de votre uncle. Now on to the next.

BEVER.

The ingenious and erudite Mr. Rust.

B 2 YOUNGER.

YOUNGER.

What, old Martin, the medal-monger?

BEVER.

The fame, and my rival in Juliet.

YOUNGER.

Rival! what, Ruft? why fhe's too modern for **him** by a couple of centuries, Martin! why he likes no heads but upon coins. Marry'd! the mummy! Why 'tis not above a fortnight ago that I faw **him** making love to the figure without a nofe, in Somerfet-Gardens: I caught him ftroaking the marble plaits of her gown, and afked him if he was not afhamed to take fuch liberties with ladies in public.

BEVER.

What an inconftant old fcoundrel it is.

YOUNGER.

Oh, a Dorimant. But how came this about? what could occafion the change? was it in the power of flefh and blood to feduce this adorer of virtù from his marble and porphyry?

BEVER.

Juliet has done it; **and** what will furprize you, his tafte **was** a bawd to the bufinefs.

YOUNGER.

YOUNGER.

Prythee explain.

BEVER.

Juliet met him laſt week at her uncle's: he was a little pleaſed with the Greek of her profile; but on a cloſer enquiry, he found the turn-up of her noſe too exactly reſemble the buſt of the princeſs Popæa.

YOUNGER.

The chaſte moiety of the amiable Nero.

BEVER.

The ſame.

YOUNGER.

Oh, the deuce! then your buſineſs was done in an inſtant.

BEVER.

Immediately. In favour of the tip, he offered chart blanche for the reſt of the figure, which (as you may ſuppoſe) was inſtantly caught at.

YOUNGER.

Doubtleſs. But who have we here?

BEVER.

This is one of Lofty's companions, a Weſt-Indian of an over-grown fortune. He ſaves me the trouble of a portrait. This is Sir Peter Pepperpot.

Enter

Enter Sir PETER PEPPERPOT *and two blacks.*

Sir PETER.

Carelefs fcoundrels! harkee, rafcals! I'll
banifh you home, you dogs! you fhall
back, and broil in the fun. Mr. Bever,
your humble; Sir, I am your entirely devoted.

BEVER.

You feem mov'd; what has been the
matter, Sir Peter?

Sir PETER.

Matter! why I am invited to dinner on
a barbicu, and the villains have forgot my
bottle of chian.

YOUNGER.

Unpardonable.

Sir PETER.

Ay, this country has fpoil'd them; this
fame chriftening will ruin the colonies.---
Well, dear Bever, rare news, boy; our
fleet is arriv'd from the Weft.

BEVER.

It is?

Sir PETER.

Ay, lad; and a glorious cargo of turtle. It was lucky I went to Brighthelm-
ftone; I nick'd the time to a hair; thin as
a lath,

a lath, and a ftomach as fharp as a fhark's:
Never was in finer condition for feeding.

BEVER.

Have you a large importation, Sir Peter?

Sir PETER.

Nine; but feven in excellent order: The
captain affures me they greatly gain'd
ground on the voyage.

BEVER.

How do you difpofe of them?

Sir PETER.

Four to Cornhill, three to Almack's, and
the two fickly ones I fhall fend to my bo-
rough in Yorkfhire.

YOUNGER.

Ay! what, have the provincials a relifh
for turtle?

Sir PETER.

Sir, it is amazing how this country im-
proves in turtle and turnpikes; to which
(give me leave to fay) we, from our part
of the world, have not a little contributed.
Why formerly, Sir, a brace of bucks on
the mayor's annual day was thought a
pretty moderate bleffing. But we, Sir,
have polifh'd their palates: Why, Sir, not
the meaneft member of my corporation but
can diftinguifh the pafh from the pee.

YOUNGER.

YOUNGER.

Indeed!

Sir PETER.

Ay, and fever the green from the fhell, with the fkill of the ableft anatomift.

YOUNGER.

And they are fond of it?

Sir PETER.

Oh, that the confumption will tell you. The ftated allowance is fix pounds to an alderman, and five to each of their wives.

BEVER.

A plentiful provifion.

Sir PETER.

But there **was** never known any wafte: The mayor, recorder, and rector, are permitted to eat as much as they pleafe.

YOUNGER.

The entertainment is pretty expenfive.

Sir PETER.

Land-carriage and all. But **I** contriv'd to fmuggle the laft that I fent them.

BEVER.

Smuggle! I don't underftand you.

Sir PETER.

Why, Sir, the rafcally coachman had always charged me five pounds for the carriage. Damn'd dear! Now **my** cook go-

ing

ing at the fame time into the country, I
made him clap a capuchin upon the turtle, and for thirty fhillings put him an in-
fide paffenger in the Doncafter Fly.

YOUNGER.

A happy expedient.

BEVER.

Oh, Sir Peter has infinite humour.

Sir PETER.

Yes, but the frolick had like to have
prov'd fatal.

YOUNGER.

How fo?

Sir PETER.

The maid at the Rummer at Hatfield
popp'd her head into the coach to know
if the company would have any breakfaft:
Ecod, the turtle, Sir, laid hold of her nofe,
and flapp'd her face with his fins, till the
poor devil fell into a fit. Ha, ha, ha.

YOUNGER.

Oh, an abfolute Rabelais.

BEVER.

What, I reckon, Sir Peter, you are going to the Square?

Sir PETER.

Yes; I extremely admire Sir Thomas:
You know this is his day of affembly; I

C   fuppofe

fuppofe you will be there : I can tell you, you are a wonderful favourite.

BEVER.

Am I ?

Sir PETER.

He fays, your natural genius is fine ; and when polifh'd by his cultivation will furprize and aftonifh the world.

BEVER.

I hope, Sir, I fhall have your voice with the public.

Sir PETER.

Mine ! O fye, Mr. Bever.

BEVER.

Come, come, you are no inconfiderable patron.

Sir PETER.

He, he, he. Can't fay but I love to encourage the arts.

BEVER.

And have contributed largely yourfelf.

YOUNGER.

What, is Sir Peter an author ?

Sir PETER.

O fye ! what me ? a mere dabbler ; have blotted my fingers, 'tis true. Some fonnets, that have not been thought wanting in falt.

BEVER.

And your epigrams,

Sir

Sir PETER.

Not entirely without point.

BEVER.

But come, Sir Peter, the love of the arts is not the fole caufe of your vifits to the houfe you are going to.

Sir PETER.

I don't underftand you.

BEVER.

Mifs Juliet, the niece.

Sir PETER.

O fye! what chance have I there? Indeed if lady Pepperpot fhould happen to pop off---

BEVER.

I don't know that. You are, Sir Peter, a dangerous man; and were I a father, or uncle, I fhould not be a little fhy of your vifits.

Sir PETER.

Pfha! dear Bever, you banter.

BEVER.

And (unlefs I am extremely out in my guefs) that lady---

Sir PETER.

Hey! what, what, dear Bever?

BEVER.

But if you fhould betray me---

C 2 Sir

Sir PETER.

May I never eat a bit of green fat, if I do.

BEVER.

Hints have been dropp'd.

Sir PETER.

The devil! come a little this way.

BEVER.

Well made ; not robuſt and gigantic, 'tis true, but extremely genteel.

Sir PETER.

Indeed !

BEVER.

Features, not entirely regular; but mark-ing, with an air now, ſuperior ; greatly above the--- you underſtand me ?

Sir PETER.

Perfectly. Something noble ; expreſſive of---faſhion.

BEVER.

Right.

Sir PETER.

Yes, I have been frequently told ſo.

BEVER.

Not an abſolute wit; but ſomething in-finitely better: An enjouement, a ſpirit, a--

Sir PETER.

Gaiety. I was ever ſo, from a child.

BEVER.

BEVER.

In short, your dress, addrefs, with a
thoufand other particulars that at prefent I
can't recollect.

Sir PETER:

Why, dear Bever, to tell thee the truth,
I have always admir'd Mifs Juliet, and a
delicate creature fhe is : Sweet as a fugar-
cane, ftrait as a bamboo, and her teeth as
white as a negro's.

BEVER.

Poetic, but true. Now only conceive,
Sir Peter, fuch a plantation of perfections
to be devoured by that caterpillar Ruft.

Sir PETER.

A liquorifh grub ! Are pine-apples for
fuch muckworms as he ? I'll fend him a
jar of citrons and ginger, and poifon the
pipkin.

BEVER.

No, no.

Sir PETER.

Or invite him to dinner, and mix rat's-
bane along with his curry.

BEVER.

Not fo precipitate ; I think we may de-
feat him without any danger.

Sir PETER.

How, how ?

BEVER.

BEVER.

I have a thought---but we muſt ſettle the plan with the lady. Could not you give her the hint, that I ſhould be glad to ſee her a moment.

Sir PETER.

I'll do it directly.

BEVER.

But don't let Sir Thomas perceive you.

Sir PETER.

Never fear. You'll follow?

BEVER.

The inſtant I have ſettled matters with her; but fix the old fellow ſo that ſhe may not be miſs'd.

Sir PETER.

I'll nail him, I warrant; I have his opinion to beg on this manuſcript.

BEVER.

Your own?

Sir PETER.

No.

BEVER.

Oh ho! what ſomething new from the doctor, your chaplain?

Sir PETER.

He! no, no. O Lord, he's elop'd.

BEVER.

How!

Sir

Sir PETER.

Gone. You know he was to dedicate his volume of fables to me: So I gave him thirty pounds to get my arms engrav'd, to prefix (by way of print) to the frontifpiece; and, O grief of griefs! the doctor has mov'd off with the money. I'll fend you Mifs Juliet. [*Exit.*

BEVER.

There now is a fpecial protector; the arts, I think, can't but flourish under fuch a Mecænas.

YOUNGER.

Heaven vifits with a tafte the wealthy fool.

BEVER.

True; but then to juftify the difpenfa-tion,

From hence the poor are cloath'd, the hungry fed,
Fortunes to bookfellers, to authors bread.

YOUNGER.

The diftribution is, I own, a little un-equal: And here comes a moft melancholy inftance; poor Dick Dactyl, and his pub-lifher Puff.

3

Enter

Enter DACTYL *and* PUFF.

PUFF.

Why, then, Mr. Dactyl, carry them to somebody elfe ; there are people enough in the trade ; but I wonder you would meddle with poetry ; you know it rarely pays for the paper.

DACTYL.

And how can one help it, Mr. Puff ? genius impels, and when a man is once lifted in the fervice of the mufes---

PUFF.

Why, let him give them warning as foon as he can. A pretty fort of fervice, indeed ! where there are neither wages nor vails. The mufes ! And what, I fuppofe this is the livery they give. Gadzooks, I had rather be a waiter at Ranelagh.

BEVER.

The poet and publifher at variance : What is the matter, Mr. Dactyl ?

DACTYL.

As Gad fhall judge me, Mr. Bever, as pretty a poem, and fo polite ; not a mortal can take any offence ; all full of panegyric and praife.

PUFF.

PUFF.

A fine character he gives of his words. No offence! the greatest in the world, Mr. Dactyl. Panegyric and praise! and what will that do with the publick? why who the devil will give money to be told, that Mr. Such-a-one is a wiser or better man than himself? no, no; 'tis quite and clean out of nature. A good sousing satire now, well powder'd with personal pepper, and season'd with the spirit of party; that demolishes a conspicuous character, and sinks him below our own level; there, there, we are pleas'd; there we chuckle, and grin, and tofs the half-crowns on the counter.

DACTYL.

Yes, and so get cropp'd for a libel.

PUFF.

Cropp'd! ay, and the luckiest thing that can happen to you. Why, I would not give two-pence for an author that is afraid of his ears. Writing, writing is, (as I may say) Mr. Dactyl, a sort of a warfare, where none can be victor that is the least afraid of a fear. Why, zooks, Sir, I never got salt to my porridge till I mounted at the Royal Exchange.

D   BEVER.

BEVER.

Indeed!

PUFF.

No, no; that was the making of me.
Then my name made a noife in the world.
Talk of forked hills, and of Helicon! ro-
mantic and fabulous ftuff. The true Cafta-
lian ftream is a fhower of eggs, and a pil-
lory the poet's Parnaffus.

DACTYL.

Ay, to you indeed it may anfwer; but
what do we get for our pains?

PUFF.

Why, what the deuce would you get?
food, fire, and fame. Why you would
not grow fat! a corpulent poet is a mon-
fter, a prodigy! no, no; fpare diet is a
fpur to the fancy; high feeding would but
founder your Pegafus.

DACTYL.

Why, you impudent illiterate rafcal!
who is it you dare treat in this manner?

PUFF.

Heyday! what is the matter now?

DACTYL.

And is this the return for all the obligations you owe me? But no matter; the
world,

world, the world fhall know what you are, and how you have us'd me.

PUFF.

Do your worft; I defpife you.

DACTYL.

They fhall be told from what a dunghill you fprang. Gentlemen, if there be faith in a finner, that fellow owes every fhilling to me.

PUFF.

To thee!

DACTYL.

Ay, Sirrah, to me. In what kind of way did I find you? then where and what was your ftate? Gentlemen, his fhop was a fhed in Moorfields; his kitchen, a broken pipkin of charcoal; and his bed-chamber, under the counter.

PUFF.

I never was fond of expence; I ever minded my trade,

DACTYL.

Your trade! and pray with what ftock did you trade? I can give you the cata-logue; I believe it won't overburthen my memory. Two odd volumes of Swift; the life of Moll Flanders, with cuts; the Five Senfes, printed and coloured by Overton;

a few

a few claffics, thumb'd and blotted by the boys of the Charterhoufe; with the trial of Dr. Sacheveral.

PUFF.

Malice.

DACTYL.

Then, Sirrah, I gave you my Canning: it was fhe firft fet you afloat.

PUFF.

A grub.

DACTYL.

And it is not only my writings: You know, Sirrah, what you owe to my phyfick.

BEVER.

How! a phyfician?

DACTYL.

Yes, Mr. Bever; phyfick and poetry. Apollo is the patron of both: Opiferque per orbem dicor.

PUFF.

His phyfick!

DACTYL.

My phyfick! ay, my phyfick: Why, dare you deny it, you rafcal! What, have you forgot my powders for flatulent crudities?

PUFF.

No.

D A C-

DACTYL.

My cofmetic lozenge, and fugar plumbs?

PUFF.

No.

DACTYL.

My coral for cutting of teeth, my po-
tions, my lotions, my pregnancy-drops,
with my pafte for fuperfluous hairs?

PUFF.

No, no ; have you done?

DACTYL.

No, no, no ; but I believe this will fuf-
fice for the prefent.

PUFF.

Now would not any mortal believe that
I ow'd my all to this fellow ?

BEVER.

Why, indeed, Mr. Puff, the balance
does feem in his favour.

PUFF.

In his favour ! why you don't give any
credit to him : A reptile, a bug, that owes
his very being to me.

DACTYL.

I, I, I !

PUFF.

You, you ! What, I fuppofe you forget
your garret in Wine-office-court, when you

1   furnifh'd

furnifh'd paragraphs for the Farthing-poft
at twelve-pence a dozen.

DACTYL.

Fiction.

PUFF.

Then, did not I get you made collector
of cafualties to the Whitehall and St.
James's? but that poft your lazinefs loft
you. Gentlemen, he never brought them
a robbery till the highwayman was going
to be hang'd; a birth till the chriftening
was over; nor a death till the hatchment
was up.

DACTYL.

Mighty well!

PUFF,

And now, becaufe the fellow has got a
little in flefh, by being puff to the playhoufe this winter, (to which, by the bye,
I got him appointed) he is as proud and as
vain as Voltaire. But I fhall foon have him
under; the vacation will come.

DACTYL.

Let it.

PUFF.

Then I fhall have him fneaking and
cringing, hanging about me, and begging
a bit of tranflation.

DAC-

DACTYL.

I beg, I, for tranflation!

PUFF.

No, no, not a line; not if you would do it for two-pence a fheet. No boil'd beef and carrot at mornings; no more cold pudding and porter. You may take your leave of my fhop.

DACTYL.

Your fhop! then at parting I will leave you a legacy.

BEVER.

O fye, Mr. Dactyl!

PUFF.

Let him alone.

DACTYL.

Pray, gentlemen, let me do myfelf juftice.

BEVER.

Younger, reftrain the publifher's fire.

YOUNGER.

Fie, gentlemen, fuch an illiberal combat: it is a fcandal to the republic of letters.

BEVER.

Mr. Dactyl, an old man, a mechanic, beneath---

DAC-

DACTYL.

Sir, I am calm; that thought has re-
ftor'd me. To your infignificancy you are
indebted for fafety. But what my genero-
fity has faved, my pen fhall deftroy.

PUFF.

Then you muft get fomebody to mend it.

DACTYL.

Adieu!

PUFF.

Farewell!   [*Exeunt feverally.*

BEVER.

Ha, ha, ha! come, let us along to the
fquare.

Blockheads with reafon wicked wits abhor,
But dunce with dunce is barb'rous civil war.

END of the FIRST ACT.

ACT

ACT II. *Scene continues.*

Enter BEVER *and* YOUNGER.

YOUNGER.

POOR Dactyl! and dwells such mighty
rage in little men? I hope there is no
danger of bloodshed.

BEVER.

Oh, not in the least : The gens vatum,
the nation of poets, though an irritable,
are yet a placable people. Their mutual
interests will soon bring them together
again.

YOUNGER.

But shall not we be late ? the critical se-
nate is by this time assembled.

BEVER.

I warrant you, frequent and full ; where
Stately Bufo, puff'd by ev'ry quill,
Sits like Apollo, on his forked hill.

E   But

But you know I muſt wait for Miſs Lofty ;
I am **now** totally directed by her ; ſhe
gives me the key to all Sir Thomas's foi-
bles, and preſcribes the moſt proper method to feed them ; but what good purpoſe
that will produce---

YOUNGER.

Is ſhe clever, adroit ?

B.EVER.

Doubtleſs.   I like your aſking the queſ-
tion **of me.**

YOUNGER.

Then pay an implicit obedience : The
ladies, in theſe caſes, generally know what
they are **about.** The door opens.

BEVER.

It is Juliet, and with her old Ruſt. Enter, Frank : You know the knight, ſo no
introduction is wanted. [*Exit* Younger.]
I ſhould be glad to hear this reverend piece
of lumber make love ; the courtſhip muſt
certainly be curious.   Good manners ſtand
by ; by your leave I will liſten a little. [Be-
ver *retires.*]

Enter JULIET *and* RUST.

JULIET.

And your collection is large?

RUST.

RUST.

Moft curious and capital. When, Madam, will you give me leave to add your charms to my catalogue?

JULIET.

O dear! Mr. Ruft, I fhall but difgrace it. Befides, Sir, when I marry, I am refolv'd to have my hufband all to myfelf: Now for the poffeffion of your heart I fhall have too many competitors.

RUST.

How, Madam! were Prometheus alive, and would animate the Helen that ftands in my hall, fhe fhould not coft me a figh.

JULIET.

Ay, Sir, there lies my greateft misfortune. Had I only thofe who are alive to contend with, by affiduity, affection, cares, and careffes, I might fecure my conqueft: though that would be difficult; for I am convinc'd were you, Mr. Ruft, put up by Preftage to auction, the Apollo Belvidere would not draw a greater number of bidders.

RUST.

Would that were the cafe, Madam, fo I might be thought a proper companion to the Venus de Medicis.

E 2   JU-

JULIET.

The flower of rhetoric, and pink of po-
litenefs. But my fears are not confined to
the living; for every nation and age, even
painters and ftatuaries, confpire againft me.
Nay, when the pantheon itfelf, the very
goddeffes rife up as my rivals, what chance
has a mortal like me.———I fhall certainly
laugh in his face. [*Afide.*]

RUST.

She is a delicate fubject.———Goddeffes,
Madam! zooks, had you been on Mount
Ida when Paris decided the conteft, the
Cyprian queen had pleaded for the pippin
in vain.

JULIET.

Extravagant gallantry.

RUST.

In you, Madam, are concentered all the
beauties of the Heathen mythology: The
open front of Diana, the luftre of Pallas's
eyes,---

JULIET.

Oh, Sir!

RUST.

The chromatic mufick of Clio, the
blooming graces of Hebè, the empereal
port

port of queen Juno, with the delicate dim-
ples of Venus.

JULIET.

I fee, Sir, antiquity has not engrofs'd
all your attention : You are no novice in
the nature of woman. Incenfe, I own, is
grateful to moft of my fex ; but there are
times when adoration may be difpens'd
with.

RUST.

Ma'am !

JULIET.

I fay, Sir, when we women willingly
wave our rank in the fkies, and wifh to be
treated as mortals.

RUST.

Doubtlefs, Madam : And are you wanting in materials for that ? No, Madam; as
in dignity you furpafs the Heathen divinities, fo in the charms of attraction you
beggar the queens of the earth. The whole
world, at different periods, has contributed
it's feveral beauties to form you.

JULIET.

The deuce it has ! [*Afide.*]

RUST.

See there the ripe Afiatic perfection,
join'd to the delicate foftnefs of Europe. In
you,

you, Madam, I burn to poffefs Cleopatra's
alluring glances, the Greek profile of queen
Clytemneftra, the Roman nofe of the em-
prefs Popæa---

J U L I E T.

With the majeftic march of queen Befs.
Mercy on me, what a wonderful creature
am I!

R U S T.

In fhort, Madam, not a feature you have,
but recals to my mind fome trait in a me-
dal or buft.

J U L I E T.

Indeed! Why, by your account, I muft
be an abfolute olio, a perfect falamongundy
of charms.

R U S T.

Oh, Madam, how can you demean, as
I may fay, undervalue---

J U L I E T.

Value! there is the thing; and to tell
you the truth, Mr. Ruft, in that word value lies my greateft objection.

R U S T.

I don't underftand you.

J U L I E T.

Why then I will explain myfelf. It has
been faid, and I believe with fome fhadow

3   of

of truth, that no man is a hero to his va-
let de chambre; now I am afraid when
you and I grow a little more intimate,
which I suppose must be the case if you
proceed on your plan, you will be horribly
disappointed in your high expectations, and
soon discover this Juno, this Cleopatra,
and princess Popæa, to be as arrant a mortal as madam your mother.

RUST.

Madam, I; I, I---

JULIET.

Your patience a moment. Being therefore desirous to preserve your devotion, I
beg for the future you would please to
adore at a distance.

RUST.

To Endymion, Madam, Luna once list-
ened.

JULIET.

Ay, but he was another kind of a mortal; you may do very well as a votary; but
for a husband---mercy upon me!

RUST.

Madam, you are not in earnest, not serious!

JULIET.

Not serious! Why have you the impu-
dence to think of marrying a goddess?

RUST.

RUST.

I fhould hope---

JULIET.

And what fhould you hope? I find
your devotion refembles that of the world:
When the power of finning is over, and
the fprightly firft-runnings of life are rack'd
off, you offer the vapid dregs to your dei-
ty. No, no; you may, if you pleafe, turn
monk in my fervice. One vow, I believe,
you will obferve better than moft of them,
Chaftity.

RUST.

Permit me---

JULIET.

Or, if you muft marry, take your Julia,
your Portia, or Flora, your Fum-fam from
China, or your Egyptian Ofiris. You have
long paid your addreffes to them.

RUST.

Marry! what, marble?

JULIET.

The propereft wives in the world; you
can't choofe amifs; they will fupply you
with all that you want.

RUST.

Your uncle has, madam, confented.

JU-

JULIET.

That is more than ever his niece will. Confented! and to what? to be fwath'd to a mould'ring mummy; or be lock'd up, like your medals, to canker and ruft in a cabinet! no, no; I was made for the world, and the world fhall not be robb'd of its right.

BEVER.

Bravo, Juliet! Gad, fhe's a fine-fpirited girl.

JULIET.

My profile, indeed! No, Sir, when I marry, I muft have a man that will meet my full face.

RUST.

Might I be heard for a moment?

JULIET.

To what end? You fay, you have Sir Thomas Lofty's confent; I tell you, you can never have mine. You may fcreen me from, or expofe me to, my uncle's refentment; the choice is your own: If you lay the fault at my door you will, doubtlefs, greatly diftrefs me; but take the blame on yourfelf, and I fhall own myfelf extremely oblig'd to you.

RUST.

How! confefs myfelf in the fault?

F

JULIET.

Ay; for the beſt thing a man can do, when he finds he can't be belov'd, is to take care he is not heartily hated. There is no other alternative.

RUST.

Madam, I ſha'n't break my word with Sir Thomas.

JULIET.

Nor I with myſelf. So there's an end of our conference. Sir, your very obedient.

RUST.

Madam, I, I, don't---that is, let me--- But no matter. Your ſervant.   [*Exit.*

JULIET.

Ha, ha, ha!

Enter BEVER *from behind.*

BEVER.

Ha, ha, ha! Incomparable Juliet! How the old dotard trembled and totter'd; he could not have been more inflam'd, had he been robb'd of his Otho.

JULIET.

Ay; was ever goddeſs ſo familiarly us'd? In my conſcience, I began to be afraid that he would treat me as the Indians do their dirty divinities; whenever they are deaf to their prayers, they beat and abuſe them.

BE-

BEVER.

But, after all, we are in an aukward fituation.

JULIET.

How fo?

BEVER.

I have my fears.

JULIET.

So have not I.

BEVER.

Your uncle has refolv'd that you fhould be marry'd to Ruft.

JULIET.

Ay, he may decree; but it is I that muft execute.

BEVER.

But fuppofe he has given his word.

JULIET.

Why then let him recal it again.

BEVER.

But are you fure you fhall have courage enough---

JULIET.

To fay No? That requires much refolution, indeed.

BEVER.

Then I am at the heighth of my hopes.

JULIET.

Your hopes! Your hopes and your fears are ill-founded alike.

BE-

BEVER.

Why, you are determined not to be his.

JULIET.

Well, and what then?

BEVER.

What then! why then you will be mine.

JULIET.

Indeed! and is that the natural conſe-
quence; whoever won't be his, muſt be
yours. Is that the logic of Oxford?

BEVER.

Madam, I did flatter myſelf---

JULIET.

Then you did very wrong, indeed, Mr.
Bever: You ſhould ever guard againſt flat-
tering yourſelf; for of all dangerous para-
ſites, **ſelf is** the worſt.

BEVER.

I am aſtoniſh'd!

JULIET.

Aſtoniſh'd! you are mad, I believe!
Why, I have not known you a month; it
is true my uncle ſays your father is his
friend; your fortune, in time, will be eaſy;
your figure is not remarkably faulty; and
as to your underſtanding, paſſable enough
for a young fellow who has not ſeen much
of the world; but when one talks of a
huſband---Lord, it's quite another ſort of
a---Ha,

a---Ha, ha, ha! Poor Bever, how he ſtares! he ſtands like a ſtatue!

BEVER.

Statue! Indeed, Madam, I am very near petrified.

JULIET.

Even then you will make as good a huſband as Ruſt. But go, run, and join the aſſembly within: Be attentive to every word, motion, and look of my uncle's; be dumb when he ſpeaks, admire all he ſays, laugh when he ſmirks, bow when he ſneezes; in ſhort, fawn, flatter, and cringe; don't be afraid of over-loading his ſtomach, for the knight has a noble digeſtion, and you will find ſome there who will keep you in countenance.

BEVER.

I fly. So then, Juliet, your intention was only to try---

JULIET.

Don't plague me with impertinent queſtions; march; obey my directions. We muſt leave the iſſue to Chance; a greater **friend to** mankind than they are willing to own. Oh, if any thing new ſhould occur, you **may** come into the drawing-room for further inſtructions. [*Exeunt ſeverally.*

SCENE

SCENE a Room in Sir THOMAS LOFTY's
House.

Sir THOMAS, RUST, PUFF, DACTYL,
and others, discovered sitting.

Sir THOMAS.

Nothing new to-day from Parnassus?

DACTYL.

Not that I hear.

Sir THOMAS.

Nothing critical, philosophical, or po-
litical?

PUFF.

Nothing.

Sir THOMAS.

Then in this disette, this dearth of in-
vention, give me leave, gentlemen, **to di-
stribute** my stores. I have here **in** my
hand a little, smart, satyrical epigram; new,
and prettily pointed: in short, a production
that Martial himself would not have blush'd
to acknowlege.

RUST.

Your own, Sir Thomas?

Sir THOMAS.

O fie! no; sent me this morning, anonymous.

DACTYL.

Pray, Sir Thomas, let us have it.

ALL.

ALL.

By all means; by all means.

Sir THOMAS.

To PHILLIS.

Think'ft **thou**, fond Phillis, Strephon told thee
    true,
Angels are painted fair to look like you:
Another ftory all the town will tell;
Phillis paints fair---to look like an an-gel.

ALL.

Fine! fine! very fine!

DACTYL.

Such an eafe and fimplicity.

PUFF.

The turn fo unexpected and quick.

RUST.

The fatyr fo poignant.

Sir THOMAS.

Yes; I think it poffeffes, in an eminent
degree, the three great epigrammatical re-
quifites; brevity, familiarity, and feverity.

Phillis paints fair---to look like an an-gel.

DACTYL.

Happy! Is the Phillis, the fubject, a
fecret?

Sir THOMAS.

Oh, dear me! nothing perfonal; no; an
impromptu; a mere jeu d'efprit.

PUFF.

PUFF.

Then, Sir Thomas, the fecret is out; it is your own.

DACTYL.

That was obvious enough.

PUFF.

Who is there elfe could have wrote it?

RUST.

True, true.

Sir THOMAS.

The name of the author is needlefs. So it is an acquifition to the republic of let-ters, any gentleman may claim the merit that will.

PUFF.

What a noble contempt!

DACTYL.

What greatnefs of mind!

RUST.

Scipio and Lælius were the Roman Loftys. Why, I dare believe Sir Thomas has been the making of half the authors in town: He is, as I may fay, the great manufacturer; the other poets are but pedlars, that live by retailing his wares.

ALL.

Ha, ha, ha! well obferv'd, Mr. Ruft.

Sir THOMAS.

Ha, ha, ha! Molle atque facetum. Why, to purfue the metaphor, if Sir Thomas Lofty

was

was to call in his poetical debts, I believe
there would be a good many bankrupts in
the Mufe's Gazette.

ALL.

Ha, ha, ha!

Sir THOMAS.

But, à propos, gentlemen; with regard
to the eclipfe : You found my calculation
exact ?

DACTYL.

To a digit.

Sir THOMAS.

Total darknefs, indeed! and birds goin
to rooft! Thofe philomaths, thofe almanack-
makers, are the moft ignorant rafcals---

PUFF.

It is amazing where Sir Thomas Lofty
ftores all his knowlege.

DACTYL.

It is wonderful how the mind of man
can contain it.

Sir THOMAS.

Why, to tell you the truth, that cir-
cumftance has a good deal engag'd my attention ; and I believe you will admit my
method of folving the phenomenon philo-
fophical and ingenious enough.

PUFF.

Without queftion.

G   ALL.

ALL.

Doubtlefs.

Sir T H O M A S.

I fuppofe, Gentlemen, my memory, or
mind, to be a cheft of drawers, a kind of
bureau; where, in feparate cellules, my
different knowlege on different fubjects is
ftor'd.

RUST.

A prodigious difcovery!

A L L.

Amazing!

Sir T H O M A S.

To this cabinet volition, or will, has a
key; fo when an arduous fubject occurs, I
unlock my bureau, pull out the particular
drawer, and am fupply'd with what I want
in an inftant.

D A C T Y L.

A Malbranch!

P U F F.

A Boyle!

A L L.

A Locke!

Enter S E R V A N T.

S E R V A N T.

Mr. Bever.   [Exit.

Sir T H O M A S.

A young gentleman from Oxford, re-
commended to my care by his father. The
                                        univerfity

univerſity has given him a good ſolid Doric foundation ; and when he has receiv'd from you a few Tuſcan touches, the Ionic and Corinthian graces, I make no doubt but he will prove a compoſite pillar to the repub-lic of letters. [*Enter* BEVER.] This, Sir, is the ſchool from whence ſo many capital maſters have iſſued ; the river that enriches the regions of ſcience.

DACTYL.

Of which river, Sir Thomas, you are the ſource ; here we quaff : Et purpureo bibi-mus ore nectar.

Sir THOMAS.

Purpureo ! Delicate, indeed ! Mr. Dac-tyl. Do you hear, Mr. Bever ? Bibimus ore nectar. You, young gentleman, muſt be inſtructed to quote ; nothing gives a pe-riod more ſpirit than a happy Latin quota-tion, nor has indeed a finer effect at the head of an eſſay. Poor Dick Steel ! I have oblig'd him with many a motto for his fu-gitive pieces.

PUFF.

Ay, and with the contents too ; or Sir Richard is fouly bely'd.

Enter SERVANT.

SERVANT.

Sir Roger Dowlas.

Sir

Sir THOMAS.

Pray defire him to enter. [*Exit* Servant.]
Sir Roger, Gentlemen, is a confiderable
Eaft-India proprietor; and feems defirous
of collecting from this learned affembly
fome rhetorical flowers, which he hopes to
ftrew, with honour to himfelf, and advan-
tage to the company, at Merchant-Taylors-
Hall. [*Enter* Sir ROGER DOWLAS.] Sir
Roger, be feated. This gentleman has, in
common with the greateft orator the world
ever faw, a fmall natural infirmity; he ftut-
ters a little: But I have prefcrib'd the fame
remedy that Demofthenes us'd, and don't
defpair of a radical cure. Well, Sir, have
you digefted thofe general rules?

Sir ROGER.

Pr--ett--y well, I am obli--g'd to you, Sir
Thomas.

Sir THOMAS.

Have you been regular in taking your
tincture of fage, to give you confidence for
fpeaking in public?

Sir ROGER.

Y--es, Sir Thomas.

Sir THOMAS.

Did you open at the laft general court?

Sir ROGER.

I attem--p--ted fo--ur or fi--ve times.

Sir

Sir THOMAS.

What hinder'd your progrefs?

Sir ROGER.

The pe--b--bles.

Sir THOMAS.

Oh, the pebbles in his mouth. But they
are only put in to practife in private; you
fhould take them out when you are addref=
fing the public.

Sir ROGER.

Yes; I will for the fu--ture.

Sir THOMAS.

Well, Mr. Ruft, you had a tête à tête
with my niece. A propos, Mr. Bever, here
offers a fine occafion for you; we fhall take
the liberty to trouble your mufe on their
nuptials: O Love! O Hymen! here prune
thy purple wings; trim thy bright torch.
Hey, Mr. Bever?

BEVER.

My talents are at Sir Thomas Lofty's direction; tho' I muft defpair of producing
any performance worthy the attention of fo
compleat a judge of the elegant arts.

Sir THOMAS.

Too modeft, good Mr. Bever. Well, Mr.
Ruft, any new acquifition, fince our laft
meeting, to your matchlefs collection?

RUST.

RUST.

Why, Sir Thomas, I have both loſt and gain'd ſince I ſaw you.

Sir THOMAS.

Loſt! I am ſorry for that.

RUST.

The curious ſarcophagus, that was ſent me from Naples by Signior Belloni----

Sir THOMAS.

You mean the urn that was ſuppos'd to contain the duſt of Agrippa!

RUST.

Suppos'd! no doubt but it did.

Sir THOMAS.

I hope no ſiniſter accident to that ineſtible relic of Rome.

RUST,

It's gone,

Sir THOMAS.

Gone! oh, illiberal! What, ſtolen, I ſuppoſe, by ſome connoiſſeur?

RUST.

Worſe, worſe! a prey, a martyr to ignorance: A houſemaid that I hir'd laſt week miſtook it for a broken green chamber-pot, and ſent it away in the duſt-cart.

Sir THOMAS.

She merits impaling. Oh, the Hun!

DAC-

DACTYL.

The Vandal !

ALL.

The Visigoth !

RUST.

But I have this day acquir'd a treasure that will in some measure make me amends.

Sir THOMAS.

Indeed ! what can that be ?

PUFF.

That must be something curious, indeed.

RUST.

It has cost me infinite trouble to get it.

DACTYL.

Great rarities are not had without pains.

RUST.

It is three months ago since I got the first scent of it, and I have been ever since on the hunt ; but all to no purpose.

Sir THOMAS.

I am quite upon thorns till I see it.

RUST.

And yesterday, when I had given it over, when all my hopes were grown desperate, it fell into my hands, by the most unexpected and wonderful accident.

Sir THOMAS.

Quod optanti divum promittere nemo
Auderet, volvenda dies en attulit ultro.
Mr. Bever, you remark my quotation ?

BEVER.

BEVER.

Moſt happy.   Oh, Sir, nothing you ſay can be loſt.

RUST.

I have brought it here in my pocket ; I am no churl ; I love to pleaſure my friends.

Sir THOMAS.

You are, Mr. Ruſt, extremely obliging.

ALL.

Very kind, very obliging indeed.

RUST.

It was not much hurt by the fire.

Sir THOMAS.

Very fortunate.

RUST.

The edges are foil'd by the link ; but many of the letters are exceedingly legible.

Sir ROGER.

A li--ttle roo--m, if you p--leaſe.

RUST.

Here it is ; the precious remains of the very North-Briton that was burnt at the Royal-Exchange.

Sir THOMAS.

Number forty-five ?

RUST.

The ſame.

BEVER.

You are a lucky man, Mr. Ruſt.

7

RUST.

RUST.

I think so. But, Gentlemen, I hope I need not give you a caution: Hush--silence ---no words on this matter.

DACTYL.

You may depend upon us.

RUST.

For as the paper has not suffer'd the law, I don't know whether they may not seize it again.

Sir THOMAS.

With us you are safe, Mr. Rust. Well, young gentleman, you see we cultivate all branches of science.

BEVER.

Amazing, indeed! But when we consider you, Sir Thomas, as the directing, the ruling planet, our wonder subsides in an instant. Science first saw the day with Socrates in the Attic portico; her early years were spent with Tully in the Tusculan shade; but her ripe, maturer hours, she enjoys with Sir Thomas Lofty, near Cavendish-Square.

Sir THOMAS.

The most classical compliment I ever receiv'd. Gentlemen, a philosophical repast attends your acceptance within. Sir Roger, you'll lead the way. [*Exeunt all but* Sir Thomas *and* Bever.] Mr. Bever, may I beg your ear for a moment. Mr. Bever, the

H friend-

friendſhip I have for your father ſecur'd you
at firſt a gracious reception from me ; but
what I then paid to an old obligation, is
now, Sir, due to your own particular merit.

B E V E R.

I am happy, Sir Thomas, if---

Sir T H O M A S.

Your patience. There is in you, Mr.
Bever, a fire of imagination, a quickneſs of
apprehenſion, a ſolidity of judgment, join'd
to a depth of diſcretion, that I never yet met
with in any ſubject at your time of life.

B E V E R.

I hope I ſhall never forfeit---

Sir T H O M A S.

I am ſure you never will; and to give you
a convincing proof that I think ſo, I am
now going to truſt you with the moſt im-
portant ſecret of my whole life.

B E V E R.

Your confidence does me great honour.

Sir T H O M A S.

But this muſt be on a certain condition.

B E V E R.

Name it.

Sir T H O M A S.

That you give me your ſolemn promiſe to
comply with one requeſt I ſhall make you.

B E V E R.

There is nothing Sir Thomas Lofty can
aſk, that I ſhall not chearfully grant.

Sir THOMAS.

Nay, in fact it will be serving yourself.

BEVER.

I want no such inducement.

Sir THOMAS.

Enough. But **we can't be** too private.
[*Shuts the door.*] Sit you down. Your Chri-
stian name, I think, is---

BEVER.

Richard.

Sir THOMAS.

True; the same as your father's: Come,
let us be familiar. It is, I think, dear Dick,
acknowledg'd, that the English have reach'd
the highest pitch of perfection in every department of writing but one---the dramatic.

BEVER.

Why, the French critics are a little severe.

Sir THOMAS.

And with reason. Now, to rescue our
credit, and at the same time give my country
a model, [*shews a manuscript*] see here.

BEVER.

A play?

Sir THOMAS.

A chef d'oeuvre.

BEVER.

Your own?

Sir THOMAS.

Speak lower. I am the author.

H 2   BEVER.

BEVER.

Nay, then there can be no doubt of it's merit.

Sir THOMAS.

I think not. You will be charm'd with the subject.

BEVER.

What is it, Sir Thomas?

Sir THOMAS.

I shall surprize you. The story of Robinson Crusoe. Are not you struck?

BEVER.

Most prodigiously.

Sir THOMAS.

Yes; I knew the very title would hit you. You will find the whole fable is finely conducted, and the character of Friday, qualis ab incepto, nobly supported throughout.

BEVER.

A pretty difficult task.

Sir THOMAS.

True; that was not a bow for a boy. The piece has long been in rehearsal at Drury-lane playhouse, and this night is to make it's appearance.

BEVER.

To-night?

Sir THOMAS.

This night.

BEVER.

I will attend, and engage all my friends to support it.

Sir THOMAS.

That is not my purpose; the piece will want no such assistance.

BEVER.

I beg pardon.

Sir THOMAS.

The manager of that house (who you know is a writer himself) finding all the anonymous things he produc'd (indeed some of them wretched enough, and very unworthy of him), plac'd to his account by the public, is determin'd to exhibit no more without knowing the name of the author.

BEVER.

A reasonable caution.

Sir THOMAS.

Now, upon my promise (for I appear to patronize the play) to anounce the author before the curtain draws up, Robinson Crusoe is advertis'd for this evening.

BEVER.

Oh, then you will acknowlege the piece to be your's?

Sir THOMAS.

No.

BEVER.

How then?

Sir THOMAS.

My design is to give it to you.

BEVER.

To me!

Sir

Sir THOMAS.

To you.

BEVER.

What, me the author of Robinson Crusoe!

Sir THOMAS.

Ay.

BEVER.

Lord, Sir Thomas, it will never gain credit: So compleat a production the work of
a stripling! Besides, Sir, as the merit is
your's, why rob yourself of the glory?

Sir THOMAS.

I am entirely indifferent to that.

BEVER.

Then why take the trouble?

Sir THOMAS.

My fondness for letters, and love of my
country. Besides, dear Dick, though the
pauci & selecti, the chosen few, know the
full value of a performance like this, yet
the ignorant, the profane (by much the
majority) will be apt to think it an occu-
pation ill suited to my time of life.

BEVER.

Their censure is praise.

Sir THOMAS.

Doubtless. But indeed my principal motive is my friendship for you. You are now a
candidate for literary honours, and I am de-

5

termin'd

termin'd to fix your fame on an immoveable basis.

BEVER.

You are most excessively kind; but there is something so disingenuous in stealing reputation from another man.

Sir THOMAS.

Idle punctilio!

BEVER.

It puts me so in mind of the daw in the fable.

Sir THOMAS.

Come, come, dear **Dick**, I won't suffer your modesty to murder your fame. But the company will suspect something; we will join them, and proclaim you the author. There, keep the copy; to you I consign it for ever; it shall be a secret to latest posterity. You will be smother'd with praise by our friends; they shall all in their bark to the playhouse; and there,

> Attendant sail,
> Pursue the triumph, and partake the gale.

[Exeunt.

END of the SECOND ACT.

ACT

A C T III. *Scene continues.*

Enter BEVER, *reading.*

SO ends the firſt act. Come, now for
the ſecond. " Act the ſecond, ſhew-
ing," the coxcomb has prefac'd every act
with an argument too, in humble imitation,
I warrant, of Monſ. Diderot. " Shewing,
the fatal effects of diſobedience to parents;"
with, I ſuppoſe, the diverting ſcene of a
gibbet ; an entertaining ſubject for comedy. And the blockhead is as prolix; every
ſcene as long as a homily. Let's ſee; how
does this end? " Exit Cruſoe, and enter
ſome ſavages, dancing a ſaraband." There's
no bearing this abominable traſh. [*Enter*
JULIET.] So, Madam; thanks to your advice and direction, I am got into a fine ſitu-
ation.

J U L I E T.

What is the matter now, Mr. Bever ?

B E V E R.

The Robinſon Cruſoe.

J U-

JULIET.

Oh, the play that is to be acted to-night.
How secret you were? who in the world would
have guefs'd you was the author?

BEVER.

Me, Madam!

JULIET.

Your title is odd; but to a genius every
fubject is good.

BEVER.

You are inclin'd to be pleafant.

JULIET.

Within they have been all prodigious loud
in the praife of your piece; but I think my uncle rather more eager than any.

BEVER.

He has reafon; for fatherly fondnefs goes far.

JULIET.

I don't underftand you.

BEVER.

You don't!

JULIET.

No.

BEVER.

Nay, Juliet, this is too much; you know it
is none of my play.

JULIET.

Whofe then?

BEVER.

Your uncle's.

JULIET.

My uncle's! then how, in the name of wonder, came you to adopt it?

I   BEVER.

BEVER.

At his earneſt requeſt. I may be a fool; but remember, Madam, you are the cauſe.

JULIET.

This is ſtrange; but I can't conceive what his motive could be.

BEVER.

His motive is obvious enough; to ſcreen him-ſelf from the infamy of being the author.

JULIET.

What, is it bad, then?

BEVER.

Bad! moſt infernal!

JULIET.

And you have conſented to own it?

BEVER.

Why, what could I do? he in a manner compell'd me.

JULIET.

I am extremely glad of it.

BEVER.

Glad of it! why, I tell you 'tis the moſt dull, tedious, melancholy---

JULIET.

So much the better.

BEVER.

The moſt flat piece of frippery that ever Grubſtreet produc'd.

JULIET.

So much the better.

BEVER.

It will be damn'd before the third act.

2

JULIET.

JULIET.

So much the better.

BEVER.

And I fhall be hooted and pointed at where-
ever I go.

JULIET.

So much the better.

BEVER.

So much the better! zounds! fo, I fuppofe,
you would fay if I was going to be hang'd. Do
you call this a mark of your friendfhip?

JULIET.

Ah, Bever, Bever! you are a miferable po-
litician: Do you know now that this is the
luckieft incident that ever occurr'd?

BEVER.

Indeed!

JULIET.

It could not have been better laid, had we
plann'd it ourfelves.

BEVER.

You will pardon my want of conception; but
thefe are riddles---

JULIET.

That at prefent I have not time to explain.
But what makes you loit'ring here? paft fix
o'clock, as I live! Why, your play is begun;
run, run to the houfe. Was ever author fo
little anxious for the fate of his piece,

BEVER.

My piece!

JULIET.

Sir Thomas! I know by his walk. Fly; and

pray all the way for the fall of your play. And, do you hear, if you find the audience too indulgent, inclin'd to be milky, rather than fail, fqueeze in a little acid yourfelf. Oh, Mr. Bever, at your return let me fee you, before you go to my uncle; that is, if you have the good luck to be damn'd.

BEVER.

You need not doubt that. [*Exit.*

Enter Sir THOMAS LOFTY.

Sir THOMAS.

So, Juliet; was not that Mr. Bever?

JULIET.

Yes, Sir.

Sir THOMAS.

He is rather tardy; by this time his caufe is come on. And how is the young gentleman affected? for this is a trying occafion.

JULIET.

He feems pretty certain, Sir.

Sir THOMAS.

Indeed, I think he has very little reafon for fear: I confefs I admire the piece; and feel as much for it's fate as if the work was my own.

JULIET.

That I moft fincerely believe. I wonder, Sir, you did not choofe to be prefent.

Sir THOMAS.

Better not. My affections are ftrong, Juliet, and my nerves but tenderly ftrung; however,

intel-

intelligent people are planted, who will bring me every act a faithful account of the procefs.

JULIET.

That will anfwer your purpofe as well.

Sir THOMAS.

Indeed, I am paffionately fond of the arts, and therefore can't help---did not fomebody knock? no. My good girl, will you ftep, and take care that when any body comes the fervants may not be out of the way. [*Exit* Juliet.] Five and thirty minutes paft fix; by this time the firft act muft be over: John will be prefently here. I think it can't fail; yet there is fo much whim and caprice in the public opinion, that---This young man is unknown; they'll give him no credit. I had better have own'd it myfelf: Reputation goes a great way in thefe matters; people are afraid to find fault; they are cautious in cenfuring the works of a man who---hufh! that's he: no; 'tis only the flutters. After all, I think I have chofe the beft way; for if it fucceeds to the degree I expect, it will be eafy to circulate the real name of the author; if it falls, I am conceal'd; my fame fuffers no---There he is. [*Loud knocking.*] I can't conceive what kept him fo long. [*Enter* JOHN.] So, John; well; and---but you have been a monftrous while.

JOHN.

Sir, I was wedged fo clofe in the pit that I could fcarcely get out.

Sir

Sir T H O M A S.

The houfe was full, then ?

J O H N.

As an egg, Sir.

Sir T H O M A S.

That's right. Well, John, and did matters go fwimmingly ? hey?

J O H N.

Exceedingly well, Sir.

Sir T H O M A S.

Exceedingly well. I don't doubt it. What,
vaft clapping, and roars of applaufe, I fuppofe.

J O H N.

Very well, Sir.

Sir T H O M A S.

Very well, Sir ! You are damn'd coftive, I
think. But did not the pit and boxes thunder again?

J O H N.

I can't fay there was over much thunder.

Sir T H O M A S.

No! Oh, attentive, I reckon. Ay, attention;
that is the true, folid, fubftantial applaufe. All
elfe may be purchas'd; hands move as they
are bid: But when the audience is hufh'd, ftill,
afraid of loofing a word, then---

J O H N.

Yes, they were very quiet, indeed, Sir.

Sir T H O M A S.

I like them the better, John; a ftrong mark
of their great fenfibility. Did you fee Robin?

J O H N,

JOHN.

Yes, Sir; he'll be here in a trice; I left him
lift'ning at the back of the boxes, and charg'd
him to make all the hafte home that he could.

Sir THOMAS.

That's right, John; very well; your account
pleafes me much, honeft John. [*Exit* John.]
No, I did not expect the firft act would produce
any prodigious effect. And, after all, the firft
act is but a mere introduction ; juft opens the
bufinefs, the plot, and gives a little infight into
the characters; fo that if you but engage and
intereft the houfe, it is as much as the beft
writer can flatt---[*knocking without*] Gadfo!
what, Robin already ! why the fellow has the
feet of a Mercury. [*Enter* Robin.] Well,
Robin, and what news do you bring ?

ROBIN.

Sir, I, I, I——

Sir THOMAS.

Stop, Robin, and recover your breath. Now,
Robin.

ROBIN.

There has been a woundy uproar below.

Sir THOMAS.

An uproar ! what, at the playhoufe ?

ROBIN.

Ay.

Sir THOMAS.

At what?

ROBIN.

I don't know: Belike at the words the play-
folk were talking.

Sir THOMAS.

At the players! how can that be? Oh, now
I begin to conceive. Poor fellow, he knows but
little of plays: What, Robin, I suppose, hallowing, and clapping, and knocking of sticks.

ROBIN.

Hallowing! ay, and hooting too.

Sir THOMAS.

And hooting!

ROBIN.

Ay, and hissing to boot.

Sir THOMAS.

Hissing! you must be mistaken.

ROBIN.

By the mass, but I am not.

Sir THOMAS.

Impossible! Oh, most likely some drunken
disorderly fellows, that were disturbing the
house, and interrupting the play; too common
a case; the people were right: they deserv'd a re-
buke. Did not you hear them cry, Out, out, out?

ROBIN.

Noa; that was not the cry; 'twas Off, off, off!

Sir THOMAS.

That was a whimsical noise. Zounds! that
must be the players. Did you observe nothing
else?

ROBIN.

Belike the quarrel first began between the
gentry and a black-a-moor man.

Sir THOMAS.

With Friday! The public taste is debauch-
ed;

ed; honeſt nature is too plain and ſimple for their vitiated palates! [*Enter* JULIET.] Juliet, Robin brings me the ſtrangeſt account; ſome little diſturbance; but I ſuppoſe it was ſoon ſettled again. Oh, but here comes Mr. Staytape, my taylor; he is a rational being; we ſhall be able to make ſomething of him. [*Enter* STAYTAPE.] So, Staytape; what, is the third act over already?

STAYTAPE.

Over, Sir! no; nor never will be.

Sir THOMAS.

What do you mean?

STAYTAPE.

Cut ſhort.

Sir THOMAS.

I don't comprehend you.

STAYTAPE.

Why, Sir, the poet has made a miſtake in meaſuring the taſte of the town: the goods, it ſeems, did not fit; ſo they return'd them upon the gentleman's hands.

Sir THOMAS.

Rot your affectation and quaintneſs, you puppy! ſpeak plain.

STAYTAPE.

Why then, Sir, Robinſon Cruſoe, is dead.

Sir THOMAS.

Dead!

STAYTAPE.

Ay; and what is worſe, will never riſe any more. You will ſoon have all the particulars;

K

for there were four or five of your friends close
at my heels.

Sir THOMAS.

Staytape, Juliet, run and stop them; say I
am gone out; I am sick; I am engaged: but
whatever you do, be sure you don't let Bever
come in. Secure of the victory, I invited them
to the celebr---

STAYTAPE.

Sir, they are here.

Sir THOMAS.

Confound---

Enter PUFF, DACTYL, and RUST.

RUST.

Ay, truly, Mr. Puff, this is but a bitter be-
ginning; then the young man must turn himself to some other trade.

PUFF.

Servant, Sir Thomas; I suppose you have
heard the news of---

Sir THOMAS.

Yes, yes; I have been told it before.

DACTYL.

I confess I did not suspect it; but there is no
knowing what effect these things will have, till
they come on the stage.

RUST.

For my part, I don't know much of these
matters; but a couple of gentlemen near me,
who seem'd sagacious enough too, declar'd that
it was the vilest stuff they ever had heard, and
wonder'd the players would act it.

DACTYL.

Yes; I don't remember to have seen a more general dislike.

PUFF.

I was thinking to ask you, Sir Thomas, for your interest with Mr. Bever, about buying the copy: But now no mortal would read it. Lord, Sir, it would not pay for paper and printing.

RUST.

I remember Kennet, in his Roman Antiquities, mentions a play of Terence's, **Mr. Dactyl**, that was terribly treated; but that he attributes to the peoples' fondness for certain funambuli, or rope-dances; but I have not lately heard of any famous tumblers in town; Sir Thomas, have you?

Sir THOMAS.

How should I? do you suppose I trouble my **head** about tumblers?

RUST.

Nay, **I did not**---

BEVER, *speaking without.*

Not to be spoke with! Don't tell me, Sir; he must, he shall.

Sir THOMAS.

Mr. **Bever's** voice. If he is admitted in his present **disposition,** the whole secret will certainly out. Gentlemen, some affairs of a most interesting nature makes it impossible for me to **have** the honour of your company to-night; therefore I beg you would be so good as to---

RUST.

RUST.

Affairs! no bad news? I hope Miſs Julè is well.

Sir THOMAS.

Very well; but I am moſt exceedingly---

RUST.

I ſhall only juſt ſtay to ſee Mr. Bever: Poor lad! he will be moſt horridly down in the mouth; a little comfort won't come amiſs.

Sir THOMAS.

Mr. Bever, Sir! you won't ſee him here.

RUST.

Not here! why I thought I heard his voice but juſt now.

Sir THOMAS.

You are miſtaken, Mr. Ruſt; but---

RUST.

May be ſo; then we will go.. Sir Thomas, my compliments of condolance, if you pleaſe, to the poet.

Sir THOMAS.

Ay, ay.

DACTYL.

And mine; for I ſuppoſe we ſha'n't ſee him ſoon.

PUFF.

Poor gentleman! I warrant he won't ſhew his head for theſe ſix months.

RUST.

Ay, ay; indeed I am very ſorry for him; ſo tell him, Sir.

DACTYL and PUFF.

So are we.

RUST.

Sir Thomas, your fervant. Come, Gentlemen. By all this confufion in Sir Thomas, there
muft be fomething more in the wind than I
know; but I will watch, I am refolv'd.

[*Exeunt.*

BEVER, *without.*

Rafcals, ftand by! I muft, I will fee him.

Enter BEVER.

So, Sir; this is delicate treatment, after all
I have fuffer'd.

Sir THOMAS.

Mr. Bever, I hope you don't---that is---

BEVER.

Well, Sir Thomas Lofty, what think you now
of your Robinfon Crufoe? a pretty performance!

Sir THOMAS.

Think, Mr. Bever! I think the public are
blockheads; a taftelefs, ftupid, ignorant tribe;
and a man of genius deferves to be damn'd who
writes any thing for them. But courage, dear
Dick! the principals will give you what the
people refufe; the clofet will do you that juftice the ftage has deny'd: Print your play.

BEVER.

My play! zounds, Sir, 'tis your own.

Sir THOMAS.

Speak lower, dear Dick; be moderate, my
good, dear lad!

BEVER.

Oh, Sir Thomas, you may be eafy enough;
you

you are fafe and fecure, remov'd far from that precipice that has dafh'd me to pieces.

Sir T H O M A S.

Dear Dick, don't believe it will hurt you : The critics, the real judges, will difcover in that piece fuch excellent talents---

B E V E R.

No, Sir Thomas, no. I fhall neither flatter you nor myfelf; I have acquir'd a right to fpeak what I think. Your play, Sir, is a wretched performance; and in this opinion all mankind are united.

Sir T H O M A S.

May be not.

B E V E R.

If your piece had been greatly receiv'd, I would have declared Sir Thomas Lofty the author ; if coldly, I would have own'd it myfelf; but fuch difgraceful, fuch contemptible treatment !---I own the burthen is too heavy for me ; fo, Sir, you muft bear it yourfelf.

Sir T H O M A S.

Me, dear Dick! what, to become ridiculous in the decline of my life; to deftroy in one hour the fame that forty years has been building ! that was the prop, the fupport of my age ! Can you be cruel enough to defire it ?

B E V E R.

Zounds! Sir, and why muft I be your crutch ? Would you have me become a voluntary victim ? No, Sir, this caufe does not merit a martyrdom.

4

Sir

Sir THOMAS.

I own myself greatly oblig'd; but persevere,
dear Dick, persevere; you have time to recover your fame; I beg it with tears in my
eyes. Another play will---

BEVER.

No, Sir Thomas; I have done with the
stage; the muses and I meet no more.

Sir THOMAS.

Nay, there are various roads open in life.

BEVER.

Not one, where your piece won't pursue me:
If I go to the bar, the ghost of this curs'd comedy
will follow, and hunt me in Westminster-hall.
Nay, when I die, it will stick to my memory,
and I shall be handed down to posterity with
the author of Love in a Hollow Tree.

Sir THOMAS.

Then marry: You are a pretty smart figure;
and your poetical talents---

BEVER.

And what fair would admit of my suit, or
family wish to receive me? Make the case
your own, Sir Thomas; would you?

Sir THOMAS.

With infinite pleasure.

BEVER.

Then give me your niece; her hand shall
seal up my lips.

Sir THOMAS.

What, Juliet? willingly. But are you serious? do you really admire the girl?

BEVER.

Beyond what words can exprefs. It was by her advice I confented to father your play.

Sir THOMAS.

What, is Juliet appriz'd? Here, Robin, John, run and call my niece hither this moment. That giddy baggage will blab all in an inftant.

BEVER.

You are miftaken; fhe is wifer than you are aware of.

Enter JULIET.

Sir THOMAS.

Oh, Juliet! you know what has happen'd?

JULIET.

I do, Sir.

Sir THOMAS.

Have you reveal'd this unfortunate fecret.

JULIET.

To no mortal, Sir Thomas.

Sir THOMAS.

Come, give me your hand. Mr. Bever, child, for my fake, has renounc'd the ftage, and the whole republic of letters; in return, I owe him your hand.

JULIET.

My hand! what, to a poet hooted, hiffed, and exploded! You muft pardon me, Sir.

Sir THOMAS.

Juliet, a trifle; the moft they can fay of him is, that he is a little wanting in wit; and he has fo many brother-writers to keep him in

coun-

countenance, that now-a-days that is no re-
flection at all.

JULIET.

Then, Sir, your engagement to Mr. Ruft.

Sir THOMAS.

I have found out the rafcal ; he has been
more impertinently fevere on my play, than
all the reft put together; fo that I am determined he fhall be none of the man.

Enter RUST.

RUST.

Are you fo, Sir? what, then I am to be
facrific'd, in order to preferve the fecret that
you are a blockhead : But you are out in
your politics; before night it fhall be known
in all the coffee-houfes in town.

Sir THOMAS.

For Heaven's fake, Mr. Ruft!

RUST.

And to-morrow I will paragraph you in
every news-paper; you fhall no longer im-
pofe on the world ; I will unmafk you; the
lion's fkin fhall hide you no longer.

Sir THOMAS.

Juliet! Mr. Bever! what can I do?

BEVER.

Sir Thomas, let me manage this matter.
Harkee, old gentleman, a word in your ear;
you remember what you have in your pocket?

RUST.

Hey! how! what?

L

BE-

BEVER.

The curiosity that has cost you so much pains.

RUST.

What, my Æneas! my precious relict of Troy!

BEVER.

You must give up that, or the lady.

JULIET.

How, Mr. Bever!

BEVER.

Never fear; I am sure of my man.

RUST.

Let me consider: As to the girl, girls are plenty enough; I can marry whenever I will: But my paper, my phenix, that springs fresh from the flames, that can never be match'd.-- Take her.

BEVER.

And, as you love your own secret, be careful of ours.

RUST.

I am dumb.

Sir **THOMAS.**

Now, Juliet.

JULIET.

You join me, Sir, to an unfortunate bard; but, to procure your peace---

Sir **THOMAS.**

You oblige me for ever. Now the secret dies with us four. My fault. I owe him much;

Be it your care to shew it;
And bless the man, tho' I have damn'd the poet.

FINIS.